Hey, kids!
See if you can spot Santa,
Mrs Claus and Reindeer
hidden throughout
the story.

To..

You made it onto Santa's NICE list – WELL DONE!

MERRY CHRISTMAS!

Love from..

I SAW SANTA IN EDINBURGH

Written by JD Green

Illustrated by Nadja Sarell and Srimalie Bassani

Hometown World

Santa's not planned any holiday this year.
Mrs Claus says, "Shall we go to Edinburgh, dear?
You always say it's your favourite place,
but remember, the children should not see your face."

"Yes, Edinburgh! That is the best place of all!
Great sights, tasty bites, super shops, big and small."

Mrs Claus says, "Let's pack. We can head off tonight!
Remember what I said? You must keep out of sight!"

The sleigh's loaded up. They are keen to explore.
There is so much to see on their Edinburgh tour.
Through Newhaven and Leith to the zoo they go.
"I love being back!" Santa says. "Ho! Ho! Ho!"

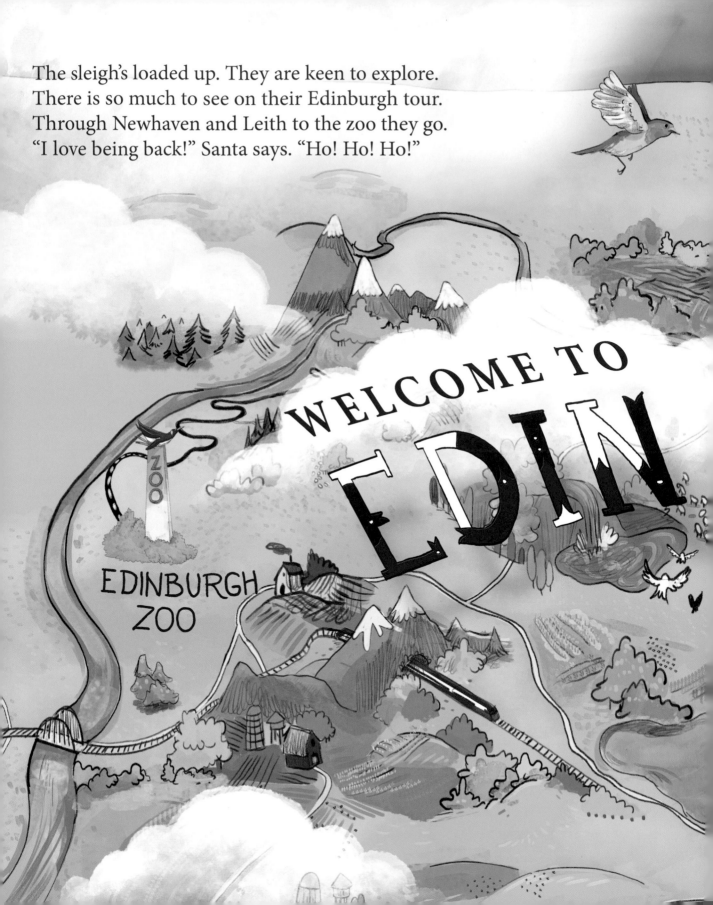

WELCOME TO
EDIN

ZOO

EDINBURGH
ZOO

NEWHAVEN

LEITH

BURGH

It's a family tradition, when they go away,
to buy a few gifts to remember their stay.

So smart Mrs Claus came prepared with a list,
she knows what to buy, and no friend will be missed.

Santa thinks buying nice gifts is quite tough.
He's feeling confused – there's just so much stuff!

His baskets soon fill up with goodies galore,
like cream cakes, pork pies, pasties and more.

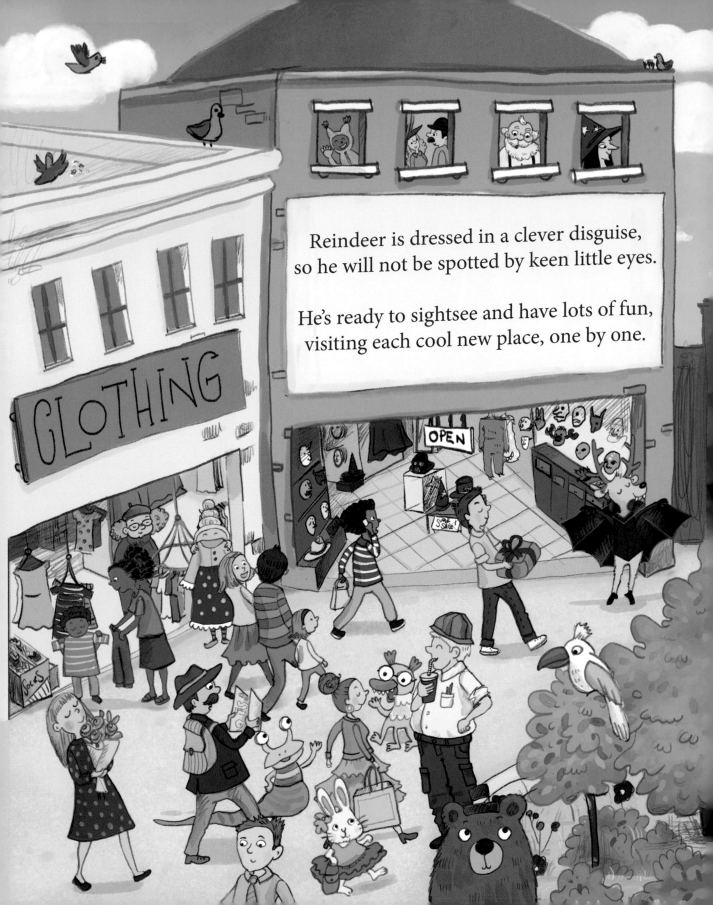

Reindeer is dressed in a clever disguise,
so he will not be spotted by keen little eyes.

He's ready to sightsee and have lots of fun,
visiting each cool new place, one by one.

The Clauses are done buying gifts for their friends,
it's time for sightseeing before the trip ends.

But at the North Pole, Head Elf checks the mail.
He opens one letter and turns very pale…

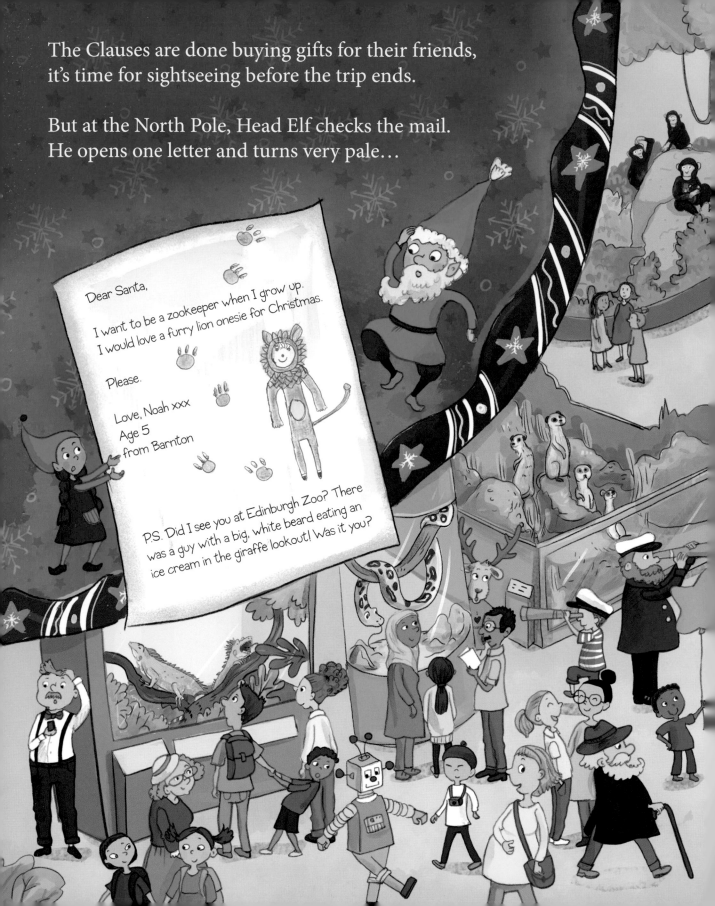

Dear Santa,

I want to be a zookeeper when I grow up.
I would love a furry lion onesie for Christmas.

Please.

Love, Noah xxx
Age 5
from Barnton

P.S. Did I see you at Edinburgh Zoo? There
was a guy with a big, white beard eating an
ice cream in the giraffe lookout! Was it you?

Dear Santa,

My favourite place in the whole wide world is the ocean! Please can I have a snorkel and flippers for Christmas? Thank you!

By the way, I was at Dunbar Leisure Pool yesterday. I didn't have my glasses on while I was swimming, but I saw someone with a big, white beard and a red-and-white bathing suit. Was it you? Please write back and tell me.

Love, Emma
Age 7
from Morningside

At home in the North, Head Elf says, "This won't do!
One sighting is terrible – now we've had two!"

Santa should really be taking more care,
it seems more children have spotted him there.

Dear Santa,

I would love, love, love a big, pink unicorn!
I drew one for you here.

Love, Bella x X x

Age 5¾
from Cramond

P.S. Did I see you at Lord Ancrum's Wood,
wearing green hiking boots and a red-and-
white striped backpack? It even sounded like
you were whistling 'Flower of Scotland'.
Am I right?

LORD
ANCRUM'S
WOOD

Reading the mail, Head Elf shakes his head.
This letter has caused him to turn rather red!

Hey Santa!

Was that you at Edinburgh Castle? I was
there with my best friend, Bobby. I know you
live in the North Pole, but it really looked just
like you sitting on a bench, wearing sunglasses
and drinking a milkshake. Oh, and we would
like new cricket bats for Christmas, please!

Bye!

William
Age 7
from Marchmont

In Lapland, Head Elf can't believe what he's seeing,
another *two* children have seen Santa fleeing!

Hello Santa,

My name is Olivia and I am 6½.
I like horse riding and would like new
boots for Christmas.

I went to the Royal Highland Show.
Did you go, too? I'm pretty sure I saw you
riding a horse while eating a hot dog!

Was that really you?

Love, Olivia
from Stockbridge

HOT

Hi Santa,

I am 8 and I would like a real duck this Christmas. My grandpa and I were watching the ducks on the Union Canal in Harrison Park when we saw a big, red sleigh on the other side of the canal. I heard the park keeper say sleighs are not allowed.

Was that you?

James
from Newhaven

The holiday's over; the shopping is done.
Edinburgh was brilliant – they had so much fun!

Now they are home, Head Elf lets Santa know,
he's been spotted a lot in Edinburgh. Oh, no!

Emma, age 7

Dear Emma,

Yes, you did spot me at Dunbar Leisure Pool! Edinburgh is my favourite place to visit. Have fun with your snorkel and flippers.

Love, Santa x

Noah, age 5

Dear Noah,

Yes, you did spot me at Edinburgh Zoo! I was on my summer holiday in Edinburgh. Enjoy your lion suit.

Love, Santa x

Bella, age 5¾

Dear Bella,

Yes, you did spot me in the woods! I was on my summer holiday in Edinburgh. Have fun with your pink unicorn!

Love, Santa x

Mrs Claus says to Santa, "I know what to do.
We can make this all good with a letter or two."

When Christmas arrives, all the children who wrote
get one extra gift, and inside is a note…

Hello little one,

On my summer break, I like getting away,
so I go to Edinburgh, the best place to stay.
There's so much in Edinburgh I like to see,
there's really no place that I'd rather be.

So keep a lookout, 'cause you never know,
if I might be somewhere that you like to go.
And if you can find time I like nothing better,
than hearing from you, so write me a letter!

Merry Christmas!
Love,
Santa

xxx